# MONSTER and CHIPS

*For James*

# MONSTER and CHIPS

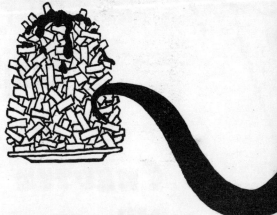

## Written and illustrated by
# DAVID O'CONNELL

HarperCollins *Children's Books*

**www.monsterandchips.com**

# CON

# TENTS

AATCHOO!

First published in Great Britain by HarperCollins Children's Books 2013
HarperCollins Children's Books is a division of HarperCollinsPublishers Ltd,
77-85 Fulham Palace Road, Hammersmith, London W6 8JB

Visit us on the web at
www.harpercollins.co.uk

1

MONSTER AND CHIPS
Text & Illustrations copyright © David O'Connell 2013

David O'Connell asserts the moral right to be identified
as the author  and illustrator of this work.

ISBN 978-000-749713-3

Printed and bound in England by
Clays Ltd, St Ives plc

**MIX**
Paper from
responsible sources
**FSC** **FSC® C007454**
www.fsc.org

FSC™ is a non-profit international organisation established to promote the
responsible management of the world's forests. Products carrying the FSC
label are independently certified to assure consumers that they come from
forests that are managed to meet the social, economic and ecological needs
of present and future generations, and other controlled sources.

Find out more about HarperCollins and the environment at
**www.harpercollins.co.uk/green**

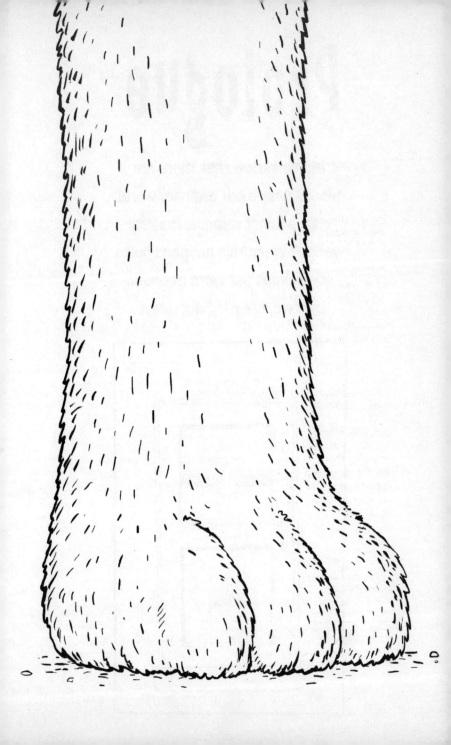

# Prologue

Did you know that there are places where our ordinary world rubs against strange, magical worlds? When this happens holes sometimes get worn between the two, creating doorways.

It can happen anywhere.
Perhaps on a street near you.
An ordinary-looking door will
appear, so ordinary that you might not
even notice it. Like the door of a diner –
just a place that sells burgers and chips.
But there might be a very special diner
on the other side of that door, with very
special customers...

# Chapter 1

# Mr Fuzzby Bixington

Joe had been sent on a perilous quest – to get chips for dinner. Mum had given him some magic tokens, or "money", as she liked to call it, and ordered him to find the finest chips in the land or die in the process. Now Joe the Fearless faced the stronghold of McGreasy's takeaway, the treasure of golden fried potato almost within his grasp. But alas! What monstrous

horror blocked our hero's path?

"Oh look, it's that squirming little bum-toot, Joe Shoe!" sneered Grotty Grace, the school bully, snapping Joe out of his heroic daydream.

Grotty Grace was one of McGreasy's best customers, and had the body to prove it. Even a fire-breathing dragon with fearsome teeth and mighty jaws would have had trouble digesting Grotty Grace. She was standing in front of the takeaway door, munching messily on a McGreasy burger with extra everything.

Joe attempted to slide past her, but

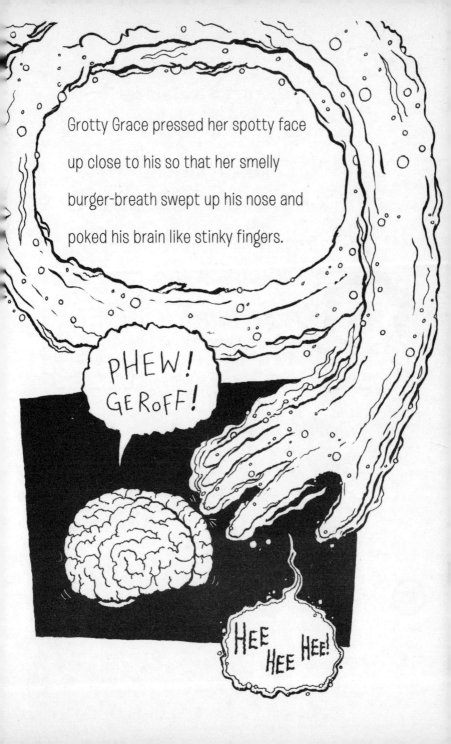

"Let me get past, Grace!" said Joe. "I'm fetching some chips for my mum."

He tried to sound like Joe the Fearless, but with his nose screwed up he sounded more like a posh duck.

GROTTY GRACE'S WOBBLY CHINS

Grotty Grace laughed, her chins wobbling like angry jelly.

GRRRRR!

AN ANGRY JELLY

"Say that you're nothing but a squirming little bum-toot and I'll let you pass," said Grace, with a menacing growl. "And if you let me have some of your chips I might not thump you."

Joe needed a plan. He didn't want to

get thumped but he wasn't going to give Grace any of his chips. He had to get her away from the door to the takeaway.

Then Joe remembered that there was a little alley at the end of the street. It looked a bit spooky but he could hide there until Grace had finished devouring her burger and gone home.

"The advantage of being a bum-toot," said Joe, summoning Joe the Fearless once more, "is that they are both lethal and invisible. Like ninjas. So I'm quite proud to say that I am a squirming little bum-toot. In fact, I thank you for the compliment."

Grotty Grace looked puzzled.

She had not expected this. No one had ever

thanked her before. She opened her mouth

to give Joe another insult. But Joe had

already gone.

"That's two thumpings you'll get now!"

Grace yelled after him.

The alley lay ahead, narrow and dark. Tall, rickety buildings loomed over it and filled it with shadow. Joe sped down its twisting path, searching for somewhere to hide. He was sure Grace would soon leave the takeaway and then he could get his chips.

But – disaster! Grotty Grace had followed him, sniffing about like a hungry wolf after a rabbit. "I know you're down there, bum-toot!" he heard her bellow. There was no escape – the alley ended in a high wall. The heavy footsteps of doom grew louder. Grace wasn't giving up. Joe was in a panic – what could he do?

Then he noticed a door he hadn't seen

before, even though he must have gone

past it. On the door was a sign that said:

FUZZBY'S DINER. Underneath that it said:

TRY OUR FAMOUS CHIPS!

Chips! He'd be safe in the diner with

people around AND get chips to take back

home. All his problems solved in one go.

Joe pulled open the door and dashed inside.

He ran straight into a pair of long, thick legs. Legs wearing green, furry trousers. Was this the latest fashion? He didn't think much of it.

"Sorry," Joe said, looking up at the owner of the legs. "I didn't—Eerrk!" The words died in his throat with a little shriek.

There, in front of him, stood a huge, terrifying, green, hair-covered creature with fangs and claws, and menacing yellow eyes. It blinked and lowered its face towards him, drool dripping from its terrible teeth.

"Oh, hello," said the monster, in a friendly voice. "Have you come about the job?"

"AAAAARRRR

# GGGHHHH!"

said Joe, which seemed the right thing to say at a time like this.

The monster blinked at him again.

"You are here to apply for the job?" he said uncertainly. "Like it says on the sign?" The creature tapped a claw on a piece of card stuck to the door. It had the words '*Help Wanted*' written on it in scrawly handwriting. "You'll only have to work an hour or so, during the busy times," he continued chattily. "And I hope you like chips. We make a lot here. Do you like them with salt and vinegar? Or curry sauce? Or perhaps with ketchup?"

The monster peered down at Joe, examining him closely.

YOU'RE A **BOY**, AREN'T YOU?

"Wh-what?" squeaked Joe, shaking.

"A boy. A child. Hoo-man." The monster said the word as if he didn't use it very often. "We don't get many hoomans in here but I'm sure they like ketchup." The monster looked at Joe again. "My name's Fuzzby, by the way," he said. "Fuzzby Bixington."

"Fuzzby?" Joe said, still slightly squeakily. "That's the name of the diner."

"Yes," said the monster proudly. "It's

my diner – a monster diner! But hooman children like chips and things too, don't they?"

"Everyone likes chips," said Joe, feeling a little more sure of himself and a bit less squeaky.

"Course they do!" said Fuzzby Bixington. "This interview has got off to a good start. Let's not stand in the doorway – come on in!"

Joe hesitated. Just then, a growl from around the corner reminded him that Grotty Grace was still on his trail.

GROWL!

Right now, being interviewed for a job in a monster's diner seemed a better idea than a double thumping. It was one type of monster or another. Joe stepped into the diner and quickly shut the door behind him.

"You've picked the right time to come, Joe," said Fuzzby. "My customers will be here soon and then I'll be very busy."

Customers? What kind of creatures were they?

"Have a look around," said Fuzzby. "I'm just going to put the chip fat in the fryer to warm up."

Joe cautiously wandered about the

diner as the monster busied himself behind

the counter. There was no one else there,

hooman or otherwise. It was exactly like

any other diner he had been in before.

There was a counter with a till, and behind

that he could see a kitchen where the

chips and other things would be made.

It was just an ordinary diner. An ordinary

diner with **a large,**
**dangerous, green**
**monster** in it.

But Joe soon realised there were

plenty of clues to the diner's monsterish

goings-on. Along the wall were several

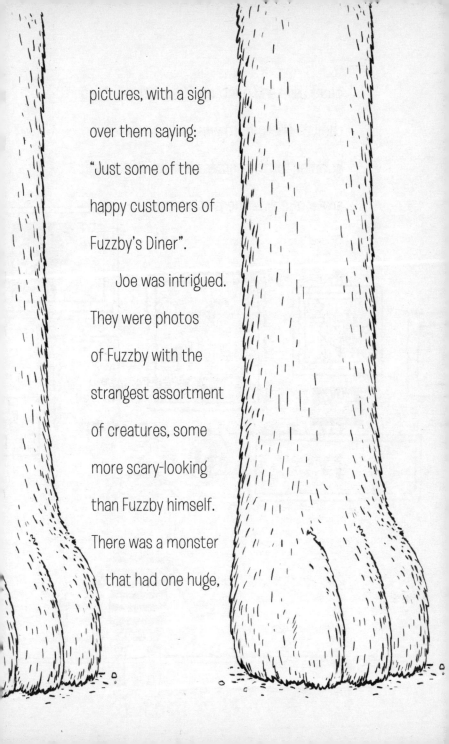

pictures, with a sign
over them saying:
"Just some of the
happy customers of
Fuzzby's Diner".
    Joe was intrigued.
They were photos
of Fuzzby with the
strangest assortment
of creatures, some
more scary-looking
than Fuzzby himself.
There was a monster
    that had one huge,

round eye and a mouth filled with hundreds of little sharp teeth. He and Fuzzby were grinning for the camera and holding a large plate of chips. There was Fuzzby

with what looked like Godzilla's smaller,

friendlier brother. There was Fuzzby with

some rocks that appeared to have eyes

and legs, Fuzzby with a well-dressed yeti,

Fuzzby with a walking rhubarb plant, and

many more. All looking cheerful,

friendly and well-fed, thought Joe.

## But fed on what?

Is there a photo of us?

They've got my best side.

"Have you cooked anything before, Joe?" asked Fuzzby from the kitchen. "What can you make?"

Joe thought for a second. "I can make sandwiches and toast," he said. "And I've made some cakes with my mum."

Joe always enjoyed helping to cook at home. Working in a monster diner could be fun.

"That's a great start," said Fuzzby. "Good, wholesome home-cooking, just like we do here. I expect you'll know some of these recipes, then."

The monster pointed to a sign stuck to the wall. It said: ⟶

Yuck! Joe was relieved to see there was no mention of 'hoomans' on the menu, though most of the dishes were still a mystery.

ORDINARY LUNCH BOX

But just imagine if he could learn to make frog fritters! Grotty Grace could be in for a few surprises next time she tried to pinch his school dinner.

JOE'S LUNCH BOX

In the kitchen behind Fuzzby, large pots bubbled and burped with purple ooze, or had brown slime dripping down their sides. A saucepan lid rose as a tentacle gingerly reached out from inside, but it shut with a clank after a quick rap from Fuzzby's ladle.

LUNCH

The kitchen shelves were equally astonishing. There were jars and tins and packets labelled with ingredients that Joe could not imagine eating. Not without them seeing daylight again pretty quickly afterwards. Pickled lizard livers. Nose broccoli. Parp tarts. Dried wartberries. A glass jar of stinky toad eyeballs blinked at him and made him jump back with a yelp.

"Watch where you're treading!" said a deep, gruff voice. "That was almost my foot."

"Don't mind the cat," said Fuzzby as a wriggling black blob with tentacles and

four eyes slithered out from behind Joe.
"Barry is very friendly. Usually."

Joe backed away from the blob nervously. "That's not a cat," he said. "Not like any I've ever seen."

"I am a cat," Barry said, insulted. "Listen: meow. See? That's what cats say, isn't it?"

"I wouldn't disagree if I were you," whispered Fuzzby as Barry nuzzled Joe's leg.

"Purr," said Barry unconvincingly. "Purr."

"Now for some questions," said Fuzzby, pointing towards a chair. Joe sat down and the big green monster sat in front of him with an official-looking clipboard. "Firstly," said the monster, "what is your name?"

"I'm Joe Shoe," said Joe.

"Correct," said Fuzzby, scribbling something on the clipboard with the stub of a viciously chewed pencil. "You're obviously a bright lad. Second question: how many hands do you have?"

Joe checked. "Two?" he said, feeling a bit unsure.

"I suppose that will have to do," said

Fuzzby, with more scribbling on the clipboard. "A spare pair is always useful in the busy times, so you might want to think about growing some more. And an extra couple of legs might be handy, while I think about it."

"Why?" asked Joe.

"You might need to outrun some of the ingredients," the monster said matter-of-factly. "They can get a little... frisky."

Before Joe could respond, Fuzzby continued the questions.

"If I gave you a bowl of uglyfish fins, floating in a soup of warm squitwater and lightly dusted with grated chinwarts, what would you have?"

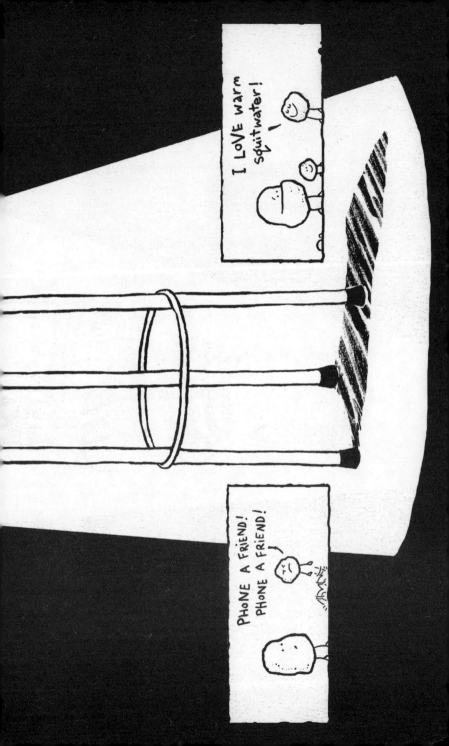

"A dodgy tummy," said Joe. He felt green just hearing about it.

"It's called Splotch Broth," said Fuzzby. "But you're technically correct," he added quietly. "Now, do you know the spell to summon the purple fire of flatulent vengeance that was belched from the giant vampire mega-toad of Urgztl?"

"No," said Joe. He was sure about that question.

"We'll have to teach you that so you can make the gravy," said Fuzzby, scribbling. "Next question: what are the twelve different kinds of sick in Surprise Stew?"

Joe didn't know but suspected his gran did, judging from her cooking. "I might need some training," he said. "But I'm willing to learn." He was warming to the idea of a job in a monster diner. And the extra pocket money would be very handy.

"Good answer," said Fuzzby. "I like a bit of ambition."

Barry sneered, "He's not so clever. How about this one: how do you get the little bubbles inside Rotten Egg Delight?"

This was obviously meant to be a hard question, so Joe decided to make up something monsterishly disgusting.

Yum! Rotten Egg Delight!

"With a good helping of baked beans and a small funnel," he said. It was worth a try.

Fuzzby and Barry looked at each other, surprised.

"Correct," beamed Fuzzby.

"Are you sure you've not been here before?" Barry said to Joe a little suspiciously.

"Last question," said Fuzzby. "What is THAT crawling up your leg?"

Joe nervously looked down, half-expecting to see the creature of his worst nightmare clamped to his ankle. When he saw what it really was he let out a huge sigh of relief.

"It's only a spider," he said.

A little spider must have attached itself
while he was outside and it was scuttling
up towards his knee.

With a yelp, Fuzzby immediately leapt
up on to a table. Barry sprang after him,
a look of terror in all four of his eyes. He
perched trembling on top of the bigger
monster's head.

"It's alright," said Joe. "Look." He scooped the little creature from his leg and carried it to a half-open window, gently letting it go on the window ledge.

Fuzzby and Barry stared in amazement.

"Did you see that, Fuzzby?" gasped Barry. "He touched it! He's saved us all!"

"You've got the job, Joe – if you want it!" said Fuzzby, climbing down from the table, peeling Barry off his head and giving

Joe a handshake that lifted the boy off the floor. "We'll ignore your almost total lack of any cooking knowledge or qualifications whatsoever. If you can handle terrifying and hideous creatures with bravery like that, then you can handle anything!"

Joe didn't need to think twice. There was adventure to be had here – adventure, monsters AND food – and Joe the Fearless was ready for it. "I'll take the job!" he said. "Bring on the vampire mega-toads!"

"Congratulations!" said Fuzzby, obviously very pleased. He lurched behind the counter again. "How about we celebrate

He got the job! HURRAY! Milkshakes for everyone!

with some chips? You can have some to

take away, Joe."

Exactly what Mum had sent Joe to

fetch! He'd almost forgotten.

Fuzzby hummed happily to himself as

he chopped up some potatoes using his

huge claws instead of a knife.

He didn't seem scary to Joe any more, especially with an apron on. Joe wondered if he was the first hooman to work in a monster diner. He imagined himself in the kitchen wearing a chef's hat, chopping up weird things at eye-blurring speed, with loads of strange creatures applauding his excellent cooking. By the time the delicious smell of frying chips wafted over the counter, Joe felt quite at home.

"All ready!" said Fuzzby suddenly.

His big green claws tipped a pan of golden, crispy-looking chips on to some paper. Joe couldn't help drooling. They

looked perfectly cooked and just the right

sort of greasy. And most importantly,

they were MONSTER-sized.

"Nice big dollop of ketchup and you'll

have a feast that would please a greedy

bellyhog on the rampage," said the

monster.

"Thanks, Fuzzby! Those look amazing,"

said Joe.

He took the wrapped-up chip parcel and tucked it under his arm. Then he remembered.

"Grotty Grace!" he moaned. "She'll be waiting outside to give me a double thumping!"

"A friend?" said Fuzzby. "Maybe she didn't notice my door. A lot of people don't."

"Definitely not a friend!" said Joe. "She just likes to hurt people, especially me."

He peered round the door into the alley. Grotty Grace was scratching her greasy head in puzzlement at the dead end in front of her.

"I'm sure the little bum-toot ran down here," she said to herself crossly.

"I'm doomed!" whispered Joe to Fuzzby. "Can't you deep-fry her or something?"

"Yuck!" said Fuzzby. "None of my customers are that hungry. Does she like cats?" he asked, with a monstrous chuckle.

As Grotty Grace peered into the gloom, Barry slithered into the alleyway behind her. A dark tentacle stretched out and tapped her on the shoulder.

Grotty Grace turned around. "What?" she said angrily.

"Meow?" said Barry, and gave her a smile full of fangs.

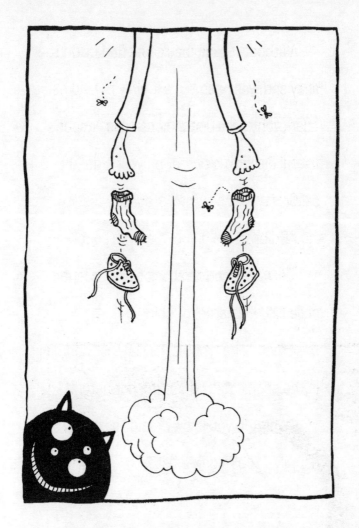

Joe had never seen anybody jump so

high as Grotty Grace.

"Eeeeeeek!" she screamed.

Without looking back, she fled down the alley and was gone.

Fuzzby gave Joe a monstrous grin. "It's useful having a monster on your side," he said.

"Brilliant!" said Joe. "See you soon!"

He waved and ran back towards home clutching his parcel of chips.

"There'll be trouble, having that hooman in the shop," said Barry. "It's not natural."

"What do you know?" said Fuzzby happily. "You're only a cat."

JOE THE FEARLESS
— MISSION ACCOMPLISHED!

# CHAPTER 2

# Milkshake Mayhem

"The first thing a monster-diner helper needs,"
said Fuzzby importantly, "is a special helper hat."

Joe was not impressed. He had run to
the alley straight after school half expecting
there to be no door or diner or big green
monster, and that he had imagined the whole
thing. But there *had* been a door, and there
was Fuzzby waiting to teach him how to be an

'official monster-diner helper'. Joe had been hoping for something more exciting.

"I feel stupid," he said, taking the bright red floppy hat. "Why has it got bells on?"

"So that customers know where you are at all times," said Fuzzby. "And I need to know where you are. You're a bit on the small side, Joe, and I wouldn't want to accidentally step on you."

He had a point. Joe would be squished into a Joe pancake under one of Fuzzby's giant feet.

Normal Joe

Pancake Joe

Joe put the hat on. He looked ridiculous.
More like one of Santa's elves than a monster's
sidekick. Barry the cat sniggered.

"What?" said Joe hotly.

"Ignore him," said Fuzzby. "He only wants
attention."

Barry flounced his tentacles huffily.
"Everyone has a right to an opinion," he said
in an offended voice. "And my opinion is that
your hooman pet looks like a Christmas tree
decoration."

"I am not a pet!" cried Joe, outraged.

"I was talking to Mr Bixington, not you, Jingle Bells!" snapped Barry.

"Now, lads, let's be civilised about this," said Fuzzby. "We've all got to work together. Otherwise I might have to add '*hot cats*' to the daily specials," he continued, glaring at Barry. "Or *Joe burgers*," glaring at Joe.

There was silence. You did not mess with Fuzzby Bixington.

Joe had a look at what really *was* on the daily specials list:

"Hash browns aren't very monsterish," said Joe, puzzled.

"It depends where the 'brown' comes from," muttered Barry.

"We had a blocked drain earlier," explained Fuzzby. "But here at Fuzzby's Diner every problem is an opportunity. Or a light snack, at the very least."

The door of the diner opened.

"Customers!" called Barry.

"Hello, Mr and Mrs Guzzelin," Fuzzby said to the open door. "And hello to all the little Guzzelins!"

But there was no one there.

Joe blinked.

"Take a seat while I get your milkshake ready," Fuzzby continued. "Pongleberry-and-gurglefish-egg-flavoured as usual?"

Were they an invisible monster family?

a voice squeaked at Joe's feet.

He looked down and saw a group of tiny creatures peering up at him. They all looked a little like rocks that had grown legs and started walking about. Two were the size of small footballs (Mr and Mrs Guzzelin), while the other four were no bigger than pebbles (the younger Guzzelins). They did not look dangerous to Joe. Not like proper monsters.

"What's that elf doing here, Mr Bixington?" said the smallest Guzzelin to Fuzzby, staring at Joe.

Barry sniggered.

"Don't be rude, Lemmy," scolded Mrs Guzzelin.

But they all gathered round Joe to inspect

him anyway.

"That is Joe Shoe," said Fuzzby, taking a mixer from a cupboard behind the counter. "He's a hooman."

"Ooooh," chorused the Guzzelins in their squeaky voices. They looked a little unsure as to what 'hooman' meant but, satisfied that Joe was harmless, they clambered up on to the table next to him to await their milkshake.

"They're very nice," Fuzzby whispered to Joe. "But there's not a lot going on in the brains department, if you know what I mean." He tapped the side of his head and winked.

Barry snorted witheringly. "They're as dense as deep-fried concrete," he said.

"Anyway," said Fuzzby, looking at Joe. "A milkshake is an easy enough task for a helper to do. All my recipes are kept in my recipe book, which only diner helpers are allowed to look at." Fuzzby pulled a giant and well-worn book from a cupboard. "Never let anybody or anything see inside it," he said sternly. "There's all kinds of magic in here. Now, I'll read out the ingredients and you get them from the fridge."

Joe jingled over to the fridge. It towered above him and he heaved open the door with some difficulty.

"Ewwwwww!" he said, wrinkling his nose.

The shelves inside were stuffed with the

most disgusting-looking objects he had ever seen. There were strange-shaped fruits, tubs of smelly slime, packets of dried-up tentacles and pots of oozing liquid. On one shelf there was a bottle with a label that said MUCOUS MUSTARD. It glowed dangerously with a sickly yellow light. On another shelf a small box with BAT HICCUPS written on its side hopped jerkily about with a squeak. A slab of *very* green cheese sent smoky fumes curling round a can of FIGBOTTOM GRAVY, dissolving the surface of the metal container. Joe thought he saw something hairy moving around in a dark crevice behind a jar labelled PICKLED TRUGGLES.

"You don't actually eat all this stuff, do

you?" he asked.

"Of course," said Fuzzby. "Don't tell me you're a fussy eater! Now, let's get started. The first ingredient we need is milk."

That was easy enough, thought Joe. He looked around, but didn't see the familiar milk carton he knew from home. He reached warily inside, trying not to touch any of the hazardous foodstuffs as he hunted around for something that looked like milk. Yuck! Was that sticky jam he'd just put his fingers into or something else? A vegetable that looked like a grumpy cabbage moved out of the way of his trembling hand with a growl.

If anything grabbed him and pulled him into the fridge, Joe just hoped Fuzzby would pull him back out again!

"I can't see any milk," he said finally, relieved to find his hand was still on the end of his arm.

Barry sighed. "There!" said the cat, waving a tentacle impatiently at a bottle with purple liquid sloshing around in it. "Honestly, Jingle Bells, get a move on! We'll be here all day."

Joe carefully picked up the bottle. The label said BRONTOSAURUS MILK. "I didn't know you could get milk from a brontosaurus," he said suspiciously.

"You need a ladder and warm hands," said Fuzzby, taking the bottle and sploshing the milk into the mixer. "And a big bucket. Next ingredient is pongleberry jam."

Joe was a bit quicker this time and found the jar easily. He took the lid off and had a quick sniff. "PHEWOOOORGHH!" he cried, coughing and spluttering. "That smells like the insides of something that's died!"

"That's because that's where pongleberries grow," Fuzzby informed him. "Inside corpses. I have to pop down to the graveyard and dig them up. It's always best to use the least fresh ingredients for maximum smelliness."

YUM-YUM!

"Yum yum!" chirped the Guzzelins hungrily.

Joe decided they did not look quite so harmless after all.

"Final ingredient: a spoonful of gurglefish eggs," said Fuzzby. "I wouldn't sniff them if I were you. They can set fire to the hairs up your nose."

Joe found a pot full of frogspawn-like gunk and quickly passed it over to the monster. Fuzzby scooped up a large spoonful of the gloopy substance and dropped it into the mixer, swiftly placing the lid on top. The liquid bubbled disturbingly, shaking the counter. The Guzzelins giggled excitedly.

"Stand back!" said Fuzzby sternly.

"Milkshakes are unpredictable beasts.

Gurglefish eggs can be a bit excitable if not

handled properly."

"I thought you said milkshakes were

*easy*," cried Joe. This was unlike any

milkshake he had ever seen made before.

"I'm going to switch the mixer on,"

warned Fuzzby. "Get ready to run for cover!"

Joe ducked behind the counter. Fuzzby

gingerly reached out a big furry claw and

pressed the mixer's start button. The

machine whirred into life and the purply-

green, oozing gunge swirled around as all the

disgusting ingredients combined together into a bubbling soup. The milkshake began to glow and the mixer trembled. Then it wobbled and jumped around the counter. The liquid frothed and boiled, trying to force the lid off the container. The mixer shook more and more violently until the whole diner shook with it.

"It's going to explode!" cried Joe from under the counter.

The Guzzelins cheered dementedly. "Milkshake! Milkshake! Milkshake!" they chanted.

"Oh dear," said Fuzzby, over the noise. "I think I might have added a touch too many gurglefish eggs."

The lid of the mixer flew towards the

ceiling with a giant SPLOT as the purply-green

milkshake burst out and flung itself over

the counter top. Fuzzby dived for cover as

revolting splodges of the mixture rained down around him. Some of it hit the floor with a hiss, dissolving the tiles with its nastiness. Fuzzby grabbed a spatula and launched himself at the milkshake beast, slapping it back into the mixer. "Get in there, you horrible concoction!" he growled.

The milkshake gurgled menacingly and for a moment it looked as if Fuzzby would have a fight on his claws. But the milkshake hadn't counted on the Guzzelins. A large drinking straw appeared from behind the counter and jabbed the angry beverage. The little rock monsters were standing on top of each other to form a short tower of thirsty menace.

Lemmy Guzzelin held the straw between his

little teeth and sucked the putrid liquid from

the counter. There was no

hope for the milkshake as

the rest of the Guzzelin

family quickly produced

straws of their own.

With a frothing cry of defeat from the milkshake and a fragrant burp from Lemmy, the last traces of the drink disappeared up the straws and into the Guzzelins' formidable tummies.

"Wow," said Joe.

"I told you," said Fuzzby cheerily. "Easy. But what's happened to your hat?"

Joe pulled the hat from his head and looked at it. There was a large hole burnt right through from one side to the other. The bells jangled forlornly.

"It must have been hit by a drop of milkshake," said Fuzzby. "You were lucky!

Any lower and it would have been straight between the eyes. It's a shame to lose a good hat, though."

Joe sighed with relief. "I'm sure I can manage without it, Fuzzby," he said.

"We'll see," said the monster. "There's plenty more action where that came from. Helping out at a diner is a dangerous occupation. You never know when the food might try and fight back, never mind the customers. A good hat can make the difference between life and death."

BLEURGH!

"Oh yes, there's never a dull moment here,"

said Barry, licking at a dollop of the Guzzelins'

milkshake that still lurked on the floor and

was trying to make its escape. "Cats love milk,

you know. *Purr.*"

"No time to talk," said Fuzzby. "Here comes the rush!"

The door opened and in walked, marched, oozed, crept and scurried the strangest collection of creatures Joe had ever seen. Had he not met Fuzzby, he would have been scared out of his wits. As it was, he couldn't quite believe his eyes. But then neither could the customers. The first couple of monsters stopped suddenly when they saw Joe, making those behind them crash into each other in a pile-up of fur, claws and tentacles.

"What is *this*?" said a monster with a

face like a scared frog, its big eyes popping

out from its scaly head and peering at Joe.

"Is it on the menu?" asked another very

small monster that seemed to be made up of

purple fur and not much else.

"I'm Joe," said Joe, becoming Joe the Fearless suddenly. "And I'm not dinner, I'm the new diner helper."

"That's right, folks," said Fuzzby, coming to the rescue. "Fuzzby's Diner is happy to welcome everyone, even hoomans! Now take your seats and we'll get serving!"

The big green monster went into action, shouting out orders for ingredients or asking Joe to fetch plates, mugs, knives and forks.

A monster with eyes on stalks like a snail and shiny red skin wanted a plate of boiled fartweed. It spat a huge gob of acidic saliva on to the plate, dissolving its food, which it

Boiled fartweed, please!

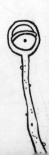

then sucked back into its mouth using a stalk
on the end of its tongue.

"That's Gordon," said Fuzzby. "Not the
best table manners, but he always clears his
plate. I like that in a customer."

Then there was Bradwell, a rotund and
friendly monster with large sharp fangs and
a pair of horns. He asked for a chip sandwich
with beetle curry sauce, then went and sat
next to the dozing Guzzelin family. From a bag
he produced some knitting.

"He's making a jumper," said Fuzzby. "He
lives up a mountain and it gets a bit chilly."

Next came Mr Jubbins, who looked like

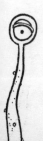

# Mr Jubbins

Mr Jubbins is a regular at Fuzzby's. You can always tell what he's had for dinner because his GIGANTIC TUMMY is totally see-through. His favourite food is SNOTBURGERS!

he was made out of blue jelly. He ate a plate of dripping snotburgers that could be seen being slowly digested inside his gigantic transparent tummy. Even Fuzzby looked a bit queasy at the sight.

Mr Jubbins was followed by a decrepit old sea monster called Doreen, who slithered in on her many barnacle-covered tentacles, bringing a wave of briny water with her. She wanted squidspawn jelly with seaweed custard.

"We'll need a mop later," moaned Barry as a crab scuttled through the puddles.

And so it went on: more strange monsters wanting stranger food; Fuzzby looking things up in his precious recipe book; Joe cleaning

tables and Barry being rude to everybody.

Despite not having a jingly hat, Joe managed

not to get squashed under Fuzzby's feet and

quickly got the hang of the way things worked.

Soon it was almost time for Joe to go home.

"You've been a great help, Joe," said

Fuzzby, beaming happily. "Now there's just one

thing left to do."

Barry cackled evilly. "And I know what it is!"

he crowed. "The toilets need cleaning! It's the

worst thing ever, especially after Mr Jubbins

has been in there! Tough luck, hooman!"

"Yes," said Fuzzby with an even more evil

cackle. "Which is why *you're* going to clean them, Barry. Joe deserves to go home early after all his hard work."

"This is cruelty to cats!" moaned Barry. "Last time I almost didn't make it out alive. Send the hooman in!" He turned towards Joe.

But Joe had already gone and was halfway down the alley.

Barry sighed. "He's a fast runner, I'll give him that," he said. "Pass the flame-thrower, Fuzzby..."

*SLAM!*

See you tomorrow, Joe!

I'd give it five minutes if I were you...

FLUSH!

WC

# CHAPTER 3

# When Cakes Attack!

"But WHERE do your customers come from?"
said Joe to Fuzzby one afternoon. "I've never
seen any monsters in the street and they
have to come from somewhere."

It was a question that had been bothering
him all day. They'd been particularly busy, with
the specials proving very popular with the
customers. Joe looked at the board.

Sausage *à la bogey* was a favourite of the round monster called Bradwell. His knitting was coming on very well. "Just got the sleeves to do," he rumbled, showing his enormous jumper to Joe. "Then I'll start work on the socks."

TIKA TIKA TIKA TIKA

He made me a balaclava!

He's the original Bigfoot!

"There aren't enough sheep in the world to make wool for those feet," Barry muttered, looking at Bradwell's gigantic paws.

Gordon, the monster who digested his food *before* swallowing it, wasn't fussy about what he ate and ordered the splatterbugs

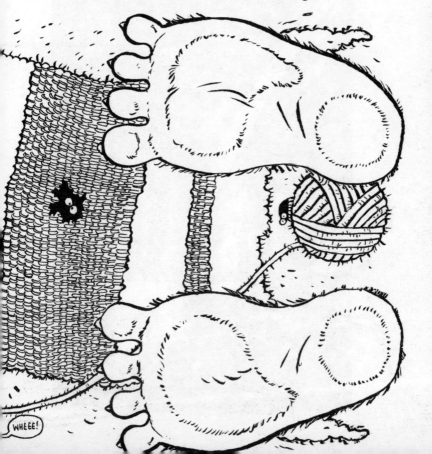

WHEEE!

and the toad tongue. There was a brief

awkward moment when he accidentally spat

on Lemmy Guzzelin, and the rest of the

Guzzelins thought he was about to eat them,

but fortunately the little rock monster

wasn't affected by the acid and things quickly calmed down.

"There's a door in the alley," said Fuzzby in answer to Joe's question. "It leads to... somewhere else. And that's where the monsters come from."

It was the kind of answer Joe's mum would give when she didn't really want him to know the truth.

"I didn't see any door," said Joe. Then he remembered that he hadn't seen the door of the diner at first. Perhaps these magic doors only showed themselves when they wanted to be seen.

"Come outside," said Fuzzby. "I'm expecting a special visitor at any minute."

Joe followed Fuzzby into the alley. There was no sign of any other door.

"Any moment now..." said Fuzzby, just as the wall opposite began to shake and tremble. Light streamed briefly from between the old bricks and with a scraping shudder a section of the wall slid back, leaving a gaping hole filled with darkness. Joe held his breath.

From the hole emerged the tip of a tree branch. Then the whole branch, then another branch. Finally an entire tree stepped out

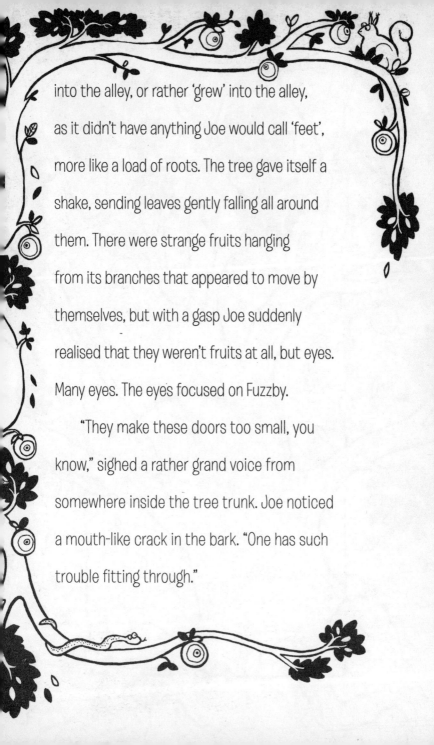

into the alley, or rather 'grew' into the alley,
as it didn't have anything Joe would call 'feet',
more like a load of roots. The tree gave itself a
shake, sending leaves gently falling all around
them. There were strange fruits hanging
from its branches that appeared to move by
themselves, but with a gasp Joe suddenly
realised that they weren't fruits at all, but eyes.
Many eyes. The eyes focused on Fuzzby.

"They make these doors too small, you
know," sighed a rather grand voice from
somewhere inside the tree trunk. Joe noticed
a mouth-like crack in the bark. "One has such
trouble fitting through."

"Afternoon, Mrs Trumptious," Fuzzby said to the tree in his usual cheery way.

"You could always saw a bit off," said Barry from the doorway.

The tree shuddered and turned its fruit-eyes on to the cat with contempt.

"I am not some common-or-garden shrub that benefits from a bit of rough pruning," said Mrs Trumptious with a haughty ruffling of leaves. "I need proper cultivation."

"Show some respect, Barry," Fuzzby scolded.

"Beg your pardon, Mrs Trumptious," said

Barry, squirming back into the diner. But

under his breath he muttered,

Fuzzby introduced Joe to the tree.

"A hooman?" creaked Mrs Trumptious, sweeping an eye-laden branch down low to inspect him. "I'm not sure I approve, Mr Bixington. Such troublesome little creatures. Far too fond of fire and axes."

"He's a good lad," said Fuzzby. "He's been a great help to me."

"He's about the same size as one of my saplings," said Mrs Trumptious. "Twig? Where are you, Twig?" The eyes peered around, looking up and down the alley at the same time.

A small girl stepped shyly from behind the tree trunk. Joe thought she looked like a girl who had fallen into a hedge and decided

she liked it so much she had brought it along

with her. Instead of hair she had a sprinkling of

tiny leaves. Her skin was papery and she had

thin, short branches that looked like arms.

"Hello,

hooman,"

she said in a

giddy voice,

staring at Joe

with curiosity.

"You're very

squishy-

looking."

"Why don't we go inside and have a cup of tea?" said Fuzzby before Joe could reply. "And some chips, of course."

"Yes, please, Mr Bixington," said Mrs Trumptious with another dramatic sigh. "I've a family of robins nesting in my canopy and it's giving me quite a headache. Mud tea would be perfect." There was a twitter of birdsong from her upper branches. "And a few worms," she added.

Oi!

With some difficulty

and several showers of leaves, Mrs Trumptious crammed herself into the diner, turning it into a temporary garden.

"Thank goodness it's not autumn," grumbled Barry, "or we'd be clearing up for days."

"Why don't you and Twig go and make a milkshake for yourselves while Mrs Trumptious and I have a chat?" said Fuzzby to Joe. "We've some important things to discuss."

Joe wasn't sure he was happy about being lumbered with this strange plant-girl, but he took Twig into the kitchen.

"Do you really work here?" asked Twig

11

dizzily. "That's amazing! I bet you know lots about making food."

"I suppose so," said Joe, though really it was Fuzzby who did all the work.

Twig looked about the kitchen at all the different pots and pans, and the shelves filled with strange ingredients. "If I worked here I'd be eating all the time," she said. "All these delicious things! Beetle-wing ice cream, chewy worm spaghetti, stinky coughy pudding, curly dog dumplings!" She ran over to a large vat in the corner and peered in. "Cold frog custard! My favourite. It must all make you so hungry!"

"Not... exactly," said Joe as the custard oozed out a bubble with a wet PARP! sound. "I usually stick to hooman, er... human food."

"Do hoomans eat different things from us?" said Twig in surprise. "How funny! What do you like to eat?"

"I like ice cream," said Joe. "Especially the type with bits of marshmallow or chocolate cookies in it."

Twig looked blank. "Marsh mellow?" she said, puzzled. "Is that a type of swamp creature?"

Joe realised that this conversation was going nowhere. "But I do like chips," he said.

"Everyone likes chips!" said Twig, brightening up. "There's nowhere else that does them as well as Fuzzby."

Joe felt very proud at this. Twig was obviously impressed that he worked in such an important place.

"They don't even make chips as good as his anywhere in Monsterworld," she added.

*Monsterworld?* So that was what was on the other side of the wall, thought Joe.

"What's Monsterworld like?" he asked eagerly.

"Haven't you been?" said Twig. "I've been to Hoomanworld loads of times. You hoomans all look the same. Squishy and miserable. And none of the trees can talk. Everyone looks different in Monsterworld, and the trees are much more friendly."

Joe listened with excitement. He really

wanted to visit Monsterworld, but it seemed as if Fuzzby wasn't keen on him going. He hadn't even told Joe about it! But why? It didn't sound like there was anything to be afraid of, according to Twig.

"I'd love to do some cooking," Twig said suddenly. She was waving a spoon around, pretending to stir an imaginary pot of soup. "Do you think I could?"

Joe wasn't sure. Twig looked like the kind of person who could set fire to herself at the bottom of the sea. "Maybe we could do something simple," he said.

On the kitchen counter a tray of gobfruit

and rat hair cupcakes was cooling. Fuzzby had taken them out of the oven earlier in the day.

"Why don't we put some icing on the cakes?" said Joe. "That's a good start. Then we... erm... you... can eat them afterwards."

"Yes!" said Twig. "Let's look for things to decorate them!"

They hunted through Fuzzby's collection of ingredients. Joe found some fly teeth, some crystallised eyeballs and a jar of fruity burpsweets.

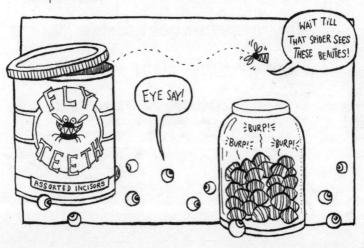

They dolloped green, gloopy icing on the cakes and sprinkled the tops with the teeth, eyes and sweets.

Twig found a pot filled with glittery powder. "It will make them all sparkly," she said excitedly. She shook the pot over the cakes, dusting them with plenty of glitter.

"I'll make a milkshake now," said Joe.

But before he could do anything, the cakes started to move about in front of their eyes, slowly shuffling around the tray. One after the other, they grew little stalks. The stalks quickly turned into little legs. The cakes began to get up off the tray and walk around, twitching and stomping unsteadily on their little feet.

"They're alive!" marvelled Joe. "What was that glitter stuff?" He took the pot from Twig and saw a label on its side. ZOMBIE POWDER, it said. "You've turned the cakes into zombies!" Joe gasped.

The little zombie cakes lurched towards them, staring with their crystallised eyeballs and gnashing their fly teeth – except for one cake that had five eyeballs pointing in different directions and walked round in a circle.

"Oh dear," said Twig. "I don't think I can eat anything that has a face."

The cakes squeaked in their little zombie voices: "BRAAIINNSS!"

"I think *they* might want to eat *us*," said Joe, grabbing a broom for defence. "Or at least our brains. If they bite us we'll turn into zombies too!"

"BRAAIINNSS!" squeaked the zombie cakes.

"Can't we do something?" said Twig anxiously. "Get Fuzzby!"

"He'll never let me back in the kitchen again if he sees this!" said Joe.

The zombie-cakes had jumped down from the counter and were slowly advancing towards them, chanting "BRAAIINNSS!" all the time.

"I heard you the first time!" said Joe.

He swept them into a corner, but the zombie cakes were undeterred. They trudged menacingly towards the two children, icing dripping from their misshapen faces like pus and leaving a trail across the floor. Joe again attempted to push them back with the broom, but a couple of the zombie cakes clung on to the end of it. He tried to shake them off, but they held on tightly and started crawling up the broom handle.

"What shall we do?" asked Twig in a panic.

Joe had read somewhere that the only way to destroy a zombie is to cut off its head,

but as these zombies were all head and no body, that might be difficult. He grabbed a large knife and sliced through the nearest zombie, chopping it into bits. Little cake body parts lay lifeless on the floor, surrounded by crumbs.

"Ooh," said Twig. "You've cut it into bite-sized portions! How clever!"

But the bits of cake twitched and grew legs of their own, making even tinier zombies.

"BRAAIINSSS!" came their little high-pitched squeaks.

"They're bite-sized, but *they're* going to be doing the biting!" cried Joe.

He scanned the shelves around him.

Maybe Fuzzby had anti-zombie powder he

could use. There was a jar labelled GUNGEFRUIT

MARMALADE. Marmalade was sticky... He

grabbed the jar.

"This is no time for a sandwich!" said Twig.

Joe started pouring the marmalade out

of the jar, the odd-shaped chunks of festering

fruit hitting the floor with a SPLUT!

"It's sticky!" he explained. "It might trap

them and give us some time to escape!"

SAVE ME!

YOU CAN
FLY, SILLY!

But the march of the zombie cakes
was relentless. Their little feet kicked
the fruit out of the way and they waded
through the sugary marmalade with crumbly
determination.

"BRAIINNS!"

Joe looked around the kitchen in
desperation. There was the great big vat of
frog custard, all cold and runny. He had an idea.
I wonder if zombies can swim, he thought.

Meanwhile, Twig had climbed on to one
of the lower shelves as the zombie cakes
crowded beneath her.

"BRAIINNSS?" they squeaked at her hopefully.

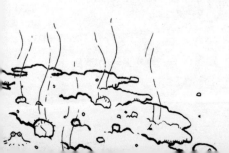

BRAINS!

BRAINS!

BRAINS!

# TWIG

Twig loves beetle-wing ice cream, chewy worm spaghetti and stinky coughy pudding. She is not as keen on ZOMBIE CUPCAKES.

"Look out!" Joe called to Twig. "I'm going to unleash the custard!"

He gave the vat a push, tipping it over on to the floor and spilling out the sickly yellow goo. It bubbled as it rolled in all directions, releasing spurts of amphibian-smelling gas. It slopped through the kitchen, sending a cold wave of frog-flavoured horror in all directions. Joe jumped on to the counter out of its reach, but the cupcakes weren't so lucky. The little zombies were swept to their doom, engulfed by the surge of custard and dragged down into its depths. The cries of "BRAAIINNSS!" sank with them beneath the surface until only harmless, soggy cupcakes were left.

"The custard must have washed the zombie powder off them," said Joe. "They're back to normal now."

"I don't think I'm hungry any more," said Twig.

Just then, Fuzzby and Barry poked their heads round the kitchen door.

"What are you two up to?" said Fuzzby, surveying the mess. "Cake, fruit and custard, if I'm not mistaken."

"And not a trifling amount!" said Barry. "Get it? I should be on TV."

"Who's this little fellow?" said Fuzzby,

ignoring the cat. The big green monster

carefully picked up a wriggling cupcake. It

was the zombie that could only walk round in

circles – and it had survived because it had

been left behind!

"BRAAIINNSS!" it squeaked at Fuzzby.

"Well, well. A zombie cupcake," said

Fuzzby with a look at Joe. "You don't see

many of those."

BRAINS!

"We had a bit of an accident..." began Joe.

"Never mind," said Fuzzby, who was in a good mood about something. "We'll keep him as a pet and feed him scrambled pterodactyl eggs. Zombies can't tell the difference between scrambled eggs and brains, if I remember correctly. What shall we call him?"

Joe thought for a moment. "We'll call him Cuthbert," he decided. "Cuthbert the zombie cake. What do you think of that, Cuthbert?"

The zombie looked at them with his five crystallised eyeballs.

he said happily.

# CHAPTER 4

# Monsterchef

Fuzzby had been in a very cheerful mood

ever since Mrs Trumptious had come to

the diner for a cup of mud tea and a chat.

Joe had been worried that he would be in

trouble after the zombie-cupcake incident,

but Fuzzby didn't seem to be bothered in the

slightest. Even Barry couldn't annoy Fuzzby,

and he tried *really* hard.

One busy afternoon at the diner, Fuzzby

asked Joe to write the list of specials for him.

It was more unusual than normal.

What a lot of strange words, thought Joe. It almost sounded edible.

Barry, Twig and the regulars studied the list with interest.

"He's gone all fancy," said Barry with a snort. "What's wrong with good old-fashioned Slime Surprise Pie, I'd like to know? It has to be *Tarte au whatsit*. I knew this would happen when *Monsterchef* came round."

"What's *Monsterchef*?" asked Joe.

"A competition to find the best monster cook," said Doreen the old sea monster excitedly, sending a ripple of seawater across the diner.

The Guzzelins cheered Lemmy as he

surfed from one side of the floor to the

other on a slice of toast.

"*Monsterchef* is shown on Monster TV.

Haven't you seen it? Mrs Trumptious is one of

the judges." Twig beamed with pride.

"That's why she was here," said Barry. "The
old stick... er, I mean, Mrs Trumptious was
letting Fuzzby know he's in the final! That's
why he's been as happy as a chuckle-monster
since. It's sick-making."

"He shouldn't be too happy," warned Bradwell, with a click of his knitting needles. "He'll need all the help he can get. The other entrants will be among the best cooks in the whole of the monster culinary community."

"Fuzzby's bound to win!" said Doreen, prodding Bradwell with a tentacle. "He never makes mistakes. Not like last time, when Boris Swampot put too much dragon chilli powder in his egg and stinkbean casserole. Poor Mr Jubbins ate one spoonful and farted himself inside out."

"Not a pretty sight," commented Barry. "And messy to sort out afterwards."

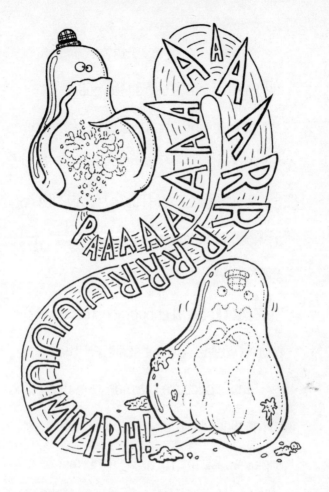

Mr Jubbins, who was never one for words,

just wobbled forlornly at the memory.

"Are you coming to watch the competition?"
Twig asked Joe. "It's this afternoon!"

At that moment Fuzzby stepped out from
the kitchen.

"No, he isn't!" said Fuzzby firmly. "It's not
a place for hoomans to go. Sorry, Joe – you're
safer here."

"But I know all about monsters now,"
protested Joe. "I'm not scared of them."

"That's because the monsters that come
to the diner are the right sort of monsters,"
explained Fuzzby, receiving a murmur of
approval from the regulars. "On the other side
of the Gate –" he waved his claw towards

The RIGHT Sort of Monsters

the alley where the hole in the wall always appeared – "are bigger, nastier monsters than any you get here. The kind that creep into your nightmares and chew your arm off, dunk it in ketchup and have it on toast. With beans. If you're lucky."

Joe was downcast. Even Barry the cat was a bit sorry for him.

"Never mind," he said with a sympathetic purr. "At least you'll get the rest of the afternoon off, as the diner will be shut. And I'll get a rest from looking at your miserable, squishy, hooman face."

Sure enough, all the monsters gradually

left so they could go and watch the competition, and Fuzzby put up a sign on the door that said  **CLOSED.**

Joe sadly mopped the seawater from the floor.

Fuzzby smiled kindly. "Sorry, Joe," he said, "but it's for the best. I've got to go now, but I'll be back later. Then I'll make you a nice big plate of chips. How about that?"

Joe sighed. "OK," he said. "Good luck, Fuzzby."

The monster grinned as he lumbered out of the door.

Joe went to put the mop into the cupboard.

Suddenly, a black tentacle stretched out from inside it and grabbed his arm, pulling him in. Joe found himself eyeball-to-several-eyeballs with Barry and Twig.

"What are you doing here?" said Joe.

"We've thought of a plan!" they whispered. "To take you to *Monsterchef*!"

Joe was impressed. Barry wasn't so bad after all.

"Great!" he whispered back. "But why are we whispering in a cupboard? There's no one else here."

"BRAAIINNSS," said Cuthbert the zombie

cake from his cage, where he was munching on some scrambled eggs

"Apart from Cuthbert," Joe added.

They tumbled out of the cupboard in a heap.

"What's your plan?" said Joe excitedly, picking himself up off the floor. "I can't wait to see what Monsterworld is like."

"It's a *really* clever plan," giggled Twig, slightly cross-eyed at the thought.

"Of course it is - it's my idea," said Barry proudly. "This is it: *we're going to disguise you!*"

"OK..." said Joe uncertainly. "What as?"

"A monster!" Barry and Twig said together.

It wasn't actually a bad idea, thought Joe, surprised. As far as he could see, a lot of the monsters who visited the diner were basically a jumble of arms, heads, teeth and tentacles stuck randomly on to a body. It couldn't be that difficult to disguise himself as another monster, could it?

"Brilliant! Barry, climb on to my shoulders," he said. "You're going to be my new head."

With a lot of complaining and a kick from Twig, Barry did as he was told. "I didn't mean *I* was part of the disguise!" he said.

Then, with Twig's help, Joe buttoned up his coat over his head to hide his face and Barry stuck a tentacle through each of the sleeves. With Barry's head and arms, and Joe's legs sticking out from the body of the

Joe    Barry

coat, they had the makings of a convincing, if

slightly wobbly, Joe/Barry monster.

"There's a good view from up here," said

Barry as he wandered about the diner, testing

out his new legs.

Joe/Barry Monster

"I wish I could say the same," muttered Joe from inside the coat. He could only just see out through the buttonholes, which meant that Joe/Barry kept bumping into things.

"No one will ever guess," said Twig with enthusiasm.

Joe walked into the door accidentally, sending Barry tumbling to the floor.

"Unless your head falls off, of course," she added brightly.

But there was no more time for Joe to practise being a monster because the *Monsterchef* competition would be starting soon.

In the alley, Twig knocked three times on the wall. Immediately, the bricks moved aside and the three of them stepped through the hole into the darkness. Joe couldn't see anything, so Twig pulled him along by his sleeve.

After a short while, Joe could tell they were in daylight again. He peeped out of the coat. This must be Monsterworld, he thought, looking around in wonder.

They were in a street filled with strange-shaped buildings that must have been built

for strange-shaped people. They had tall,

wide doors with handles meant for claws, not

fingers. Some of the strange creatures walking

around looked a bit like the customers of the

diner, but there were other kinds too, all going

about their business. A one-eyed pig-monster

walked along the street beside them, pushing

a buggy carrying a sleeping baby version of

itself. A giant fur-covered monster with antlers

growing out of its head cycled past on a

wobbly bike. A purple blob with five legs and

three heads on the end of giraffe-like necks

trotted past pulling a dog-monster on a lead.

"Afternoon," it said pleasantly. Joe's disguise seemed to be working.

The three of them stopped in front of a large building. Outside there was a queue of excited monsters.

"It's the TV studio where they make *Monsterchef*," whispered Twig. "Fuzzby must be inside already."

They joined the end of the queue, Joe/Barry trying to look as cool as it was possible to be when you had a head that wanted to go in a different direction from the rest of your body. Luckily, this was quite normal for Monsterworld, so no one paid them any attention.

They hadn't been there long when a pale, worm-like monster slithered up to the studio. It had a nasty smile filled with teeth that were like pins and it blinked at the queue of monsters with cold, ink-black eyes. It wore an expensive velvet waistcoat and left a trail of glistening slime behind it as it moved.

"It's Uncton Slugglesbutt!" said Twig. "Mum said he was in the competition!"

"He's very jealous of Fuzzby's Diner," said Barry, with a hint of pride. "He'd do anything to see Fuzzby lose the competition."

Two large, ugly monsters walked in front of Slugglesbutt. They were all teeth, scales, warts

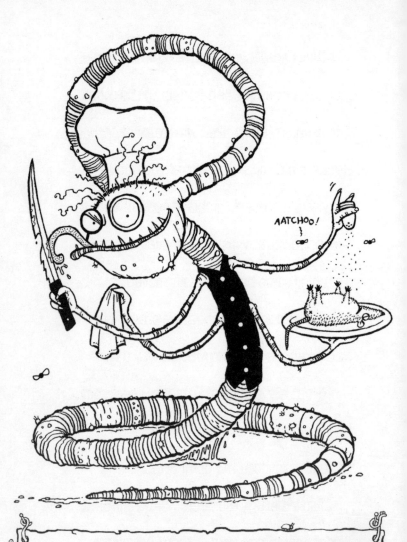

AATCHOO!

# UNCTON SLUGGLESBUTT

Uncton isn't as nice as he looks. He is a bit MEAN.
He likes food with a heart. And other vital organs,
PREFERABLY STILL WARM.

and growl. These were the type of monsters that Fuzzby had warned Joe about, the ones that liked arms on toast. He shivered and was glad he was disguised. The large monsters were carrying Slugglesbutt's cooking equipment in boxes and pushing smaller monsters out of his way. A piece of paper fluttered out of one of the boxes and landed at Joe's feet. No one was looking so he stretched his arm down and picked it up. It was a label that must have fallen off some packaging. It said:

Spoon-activated Travelling Plate

Made by Spudington Magical Kitchen Supplies.

Joe had no idea what a travelling plate was,

but he stuffed the label into a pocket.

The queue started moving.

"We're going in now," said Barry from on top of Joe's shoulders. "Everybody act normal, not hooman."

Inside the studio, a kitchen had been built for the competitors to use for cooking. Around it were several camera-monsters getting ready to film everything for TV. Joe saw that Doreen, Bradwell, Gordon and even the Guzzelins had turned up to support Fuzzby. He and the others found some seats right at the front so they would have a good view of everything.

From a loudspeaker on the wall came

the announcement that the programme was about to start, and then some dramatic music played. *Monsterchef* had begun!

A greedy-looking monster with a large green body and a number of crab-like legs tottered on to the set. The monsters in the audience cheered.

"I'm Toadly Bellybutter and I'm your host on this year's edition of... *Monsterchef*!"

More dramatic music played. The audience cheered again.

"We've three brave contestants on the show today, ready to do battle with each other for the title of best Monsterchef. Let's meet them!"

A round blue monster that looked like a balloon with four legs trotted in, lit up by a bright spotlight. She smiled confidently.

"Hello, my name's Ethelurga," said the monster. "I'm a mother of forty-three children, although some of them haven't hatched yet. I like good, plain home-cooking with plenty of stodgy, greasy bits and lots of scummy, congealed things."

The audience cheered their approval.

"She writes cookery books," Twig whispered to Joe. "She's trying to get her own cooking programme."

"For *Monsterchef* I'm going to be baking a very special cake," said Ethelurga confidently. "It's my own recipe – a weevil's food cake, with a freshly hoicked mucus cream filling, decorated with ripe, burst-in-the-mouth zitberries."

"I can almost taste them!" said Toadly,

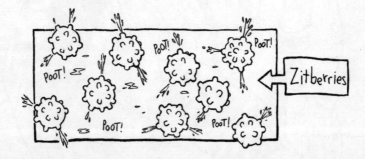

which was not surprising as his frog-like tongue had been licking a spot on his oily face. "Now let's meet our second contestant!"

"Here's Fuzzby!" said Barry, waving his tentacles as the big green monster lumbered on to the set.

He grinned at the monsters in the

audience in his friendly way, then frowned

when he noticed Barry in the front row

wearing a coat with a pair of legs sticking out

of it.

"Uh-oh," said Barry. "He's spotted us!"

But before Fuzzby could say anything, he

was given a nudge by Toadly Bellybutter.

"Erm... hello, my name's Fuzzby," he said, "and I run Fuzzby's Diner, famous for its chips."

There were cheers from the audience. Gordon, Bradwell, Doreen and the Guzzelins did a Mexican wave, which took some time due to the number of tentacles Doreen had.

"I'm going to be making my speciality: *Tarte Surprise au Slime*. Flaky dandruff pastry, filled with snot-worm nose pus. I don't want to spoil the surprise, but it involves chewy green bits and some minor explosions. All served with my famous chips, of course!"

"Hurray for Fuzzby!" shouted the

audience, including Joe and the others. Twig
showered leaves around her as she cheered
and Barry almost fell off his perch on Joe's
shoulders after a bout of energetic tentacle
waving.

"And now, please welcome our final
contestant on *Monsterchef*!" said Toadly.

The spotlight fell on the pale face of
Uncton Slugglesbutt as he slithered on
to the stage, grinning with his pointy
teeth. He looked very pleased with
himself.

"My name is Uncton," said Uncton with a
quiet hiss. "Mr Slugglesbutt to you. I like food

with a heart. And other vital organs, preferably still warm. I own the Slugglesbutt Bistro, the finest restaurant in Monsterworld. We serve the finest food for only the finest monsters. And definitely no chips."

There was polite applause from the audience. Fuzzby growled. No one was allowed to insult his beloved chips. What an unpleasant monster, thought Joe, with his nasty slimy trail and – what was that? As well as slime, Uncton was leaving behind a trickle of fine, crumbly dust as he moved. How strange...

Uncton continued, "And only *I* am a good

enough cook to win *Monsterchef*. I shall win this competition with a delicious salad of scabpox-riddled turnip, itchy-bum nettles, fried stoat's cheese and garlic-breath croutons."

"Wonderful!" oozed Toadly Bellybutter (there was an actual trail of ooze on the floor). "Now please welcome our expert judges, Mr Jubbins and Mrs Trumptious!"

"Here's Mum!" said Twig, as Mrs Trumptious the tree monster grandly creaked on to the set, followed by the jellified form of Mr Jubbins, gurgling happily. Mrs Trumptious's robin fluttered about in her branches, then decided to sit on Toadly's head for a better view.

I don't like itchy-bum nettles!

Hee hee!

"We're all ready," announced Toadly,

accompanied by a few bursts of birdsong.

"So, contestants – on your marks, get set,

The three monsters raced to their separate
parts of the kitchen and began cooking furiously,
cutting, slicing, grating and stabbing all kind
of particularly revolting and sometimes
downright uncooperative ingredients.

Joe watched through the gap in his coat
as grungy dollops of grease and sticky green
liquid flew everywhere, while hideous smells
erupted and bubbled from cooking pots and
mixers. He was glad to be there to support
Fuzzby, but was beginning to regret sitting
right at the front, near the kitchen. It
was all he could do not to faint from the
stench when one of Ethelurga's zitberries

bounced off her table and burst in front of him. He pressed his nose into the coat to smother the smell. But the audience loved every second and were soon drooling at the

sight of the feast being prepared in front of
them. Finally, after a lot of baking, stirring,
frying and hitting things with spatulas, it
was all over. A buzzer rang. Time was up! Joe
breathed a sigh of relief.

"Now it's time for the judging!" said Twig.

"Come on, Fuzzby!" said Barry nervously.
"You can do it, you great big hairball."

First to be judged was Ethelurga. Her
spectacular many-layered cake towered
over her. Each layer had a bogey-rippled
cream filling that dripped down the sides of
the creation. The top was decorated with a
scattering of red zitberries, plump and ripe
and, as Joe knew all too well, ready to pop.
It looked perfect. Ethelurga beamed proudly.
Mr Jubbins licked his lips and picked up a
knife to cut a slice of the cake. But as soon
as the knife touched it – PIF! – the sponge

disappeared into thin air! The zitberries and

cream filling collapsed to the table in a soggy

mess, splattering everyone around.

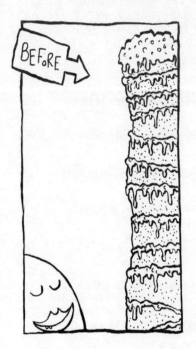

"What's happened?" shrieked Ethelurga,

horrified.

Mrs Trumptious frowned and then leant over to the table where Ethelurga had been cooking. A branch swept down and picked up an open bag of flour for Mrs Trumptious's many eyes to inspect.

"This bag is filled with self-erasing flour instead of normal flour," she said, after examining it closely. "As soon as you cut into it, it erases itself!"

The audience gasped.

"But I'm sure it was normal flour this morning," said a distraught Ethelurga. But it was no good. With no cake to judge, Ethelurga was out of the competition.

"Such a foolish mistake!" Uncton Slugglesbutt sneered happily. "I'd never do such a thing."

"What a terrible tragedy!" sighed Toadly, who loved a bit of drama. The robin on his head chirped in agreement.

"On with the judging!" commanded Mrs Trumptious. "Mr Bixington's next!"

Mr Jubbins picked up a spoon. Fuzzby's *Tarte Surprise au Slime* looked very tasty, its green and beige filling glistening in the spotlight. But just as the spoon reached the pie, the pie dish suddenly sprouted a pair of tiny legs, jumped up off the table and ran out of the door of the studio, scattering

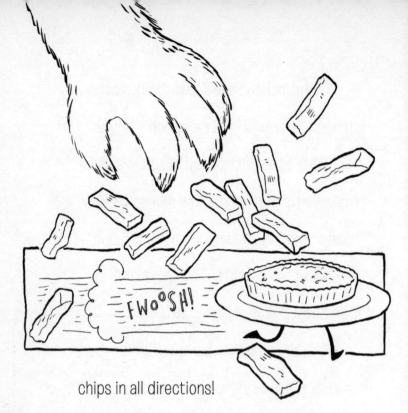

FWOOSH!

chips in all directions!

Everybody gasped again! A vanishing cake?

An escaped pie? Never had a *Monsterchef*

contest been more eventful!

"A dashing dish!" said Twig. "How did that

get there?"

"Poor Fuzzby!" said Barry. "Though usually the dish runs away with the spoon, I've heard."

Fuzzby looked crushed. He had practised for ages for the competition and now he was going to lose because of an unruly piece of crockery.

"A dashing dish?" said Joe. "You mean, a plate that can travel..."

Over and above all the other stinkiness, Joe was beginning to smell a rat.

IT'S NOT ME, DEAR.

Meanwhile, rules were rules, and if there was nothing for the judges to taste, then Fuzzby was disqualified.

"I win! I win!" said Uncton Slugglesbutt triumphantly. "The competition's over."

"We have to try your dish first, Mr Slugglesbutt," said Mrs Trumptious. "They're the rules."

"Fine!" said Slugglesbutt haughtily. "I don't think you'll find anything wrong with my food."

"CHEAT!" The word had popped out of Joe's mouth before he could stop himself. "Cheat!"

Everyone turned to look at the strange creature wrapped up in a coat in the front row.

"*What are you doing?!*" hissed Barry.

"You'll give us away if you're not careful."

But someone was up to no good and Joe
was determined to put a stop to it. He stood
up, making Barry wobble precariously, and ran
into the *Monsterchef* kitchen. Barry wrapped
his tentacles tightly round Joe's face

"Stop!" cried the cat, hanging on for
dear life.

MMMMEEEE

"I can't see!" Joe tried to say, but it was too late. He tripped over one of the camera cables and fell flat on to the ground.

With a startled *meow*, Barry shot out of the coat and went flying across the studio. The cat landed right in the middle of Uncton's salad with a huge

"Barry!" roared Fuzzby. "I thought it was you sitting there. And I bet I know who's inside that coat too. Come here, Joe."

Joe walked, shamefaced, over to where the judges and contestants stood. All the monsters in the audience gasped. What was this creature? What was it doing here? What did it mean?

"A *hooman*? In Monsterworld?" exclaimed Toadly. "I've never heard of such a thing!"

"He's with me," said Fuzzby. "But he shouldn't be! I told you not to come here, Joe. I'm very disappointed in you."

"It was my idea," admitted Barry from the salad bowl. "Well, the clever bits were."

"I'm sorry, Fuzzby," said Joe. "I just wanted to cheer you on. But I couldn't keep quiet when I knew you were about to lose to a cheat!" he said, pointing at Uncton.

"Only Fuzzby Bixington would be friends with a troublesome creature like this! We all know that hoomans are only fit for stewing!"

He ran a black tongue along his spiky teeth and Joe backed away.

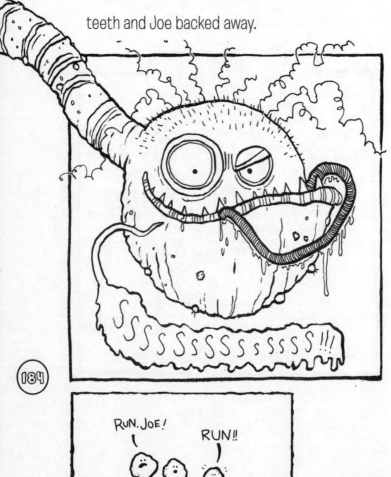

"You had better have some proof of your accusation, young hooman," said Mrs Trumptious, looking at him very sternly from several eyes

Joe produced the paper label he'd picked up outside the studio.

"This belongs to Uncton," he said. "He brought the dashing dish!"

"That could have come from anywhere!" spat the worm.

"I think if we check with Spudington Magical Kitchen Supplies, we'll find it belongs to you," said Joe. "And I also think we'll find the missing bag of flour hidden inside your velvet waistcoat. It's been leaking everywhere."

Uncton hissed at him, but Fuzzby was too quick and grabbed the monster with his big green claws. Sure enough, tucked inside the worm's waistcoat was the leaky bag of flour, dribbling the powdery trail Joe had noticed earlier.

"Well done, Joe!" said Fuzzby.

"Uncton Slugglesbutt, you are hereby disqualified from *Monsterchef* for cheating!" pronounced Mrs Trumptious.

"I'll get even with you, Bixington!" said Uncton as he slithered out of the studio to boos from the audience. "And your little hooman..."

"A shame, really," said Barry, with a mouthful of itchy-bum nettles. "He might have won without cheating. This salad's not bad." Fuzzby glared at him. "Needs some chips, of course," the cat added quickly.

"So who *has* won?" said Twig, running on to the set. "There's no food left to judge!"

"The competition is cancelled!" said Mrs Trumptious. "But we'll invite Fuzzby and Ethelurga back for the next one."

"I can see it now," said Toadly, almost overcome with excitement. "*Monsterchef: The Rematch!*"

"All's well that ends well," said Fuzzby

with a sigh. "I may not have won, but at least

Uncton Slugglesbutt didn't either. And there's

always next time. I'll even let you come and

watch, Joe. You've earned a reward." He gave

Joe a hug.

"In fact, we all deserve a reward," said the big green monster with a grin. "Who'd like a nice plate of golden, freshly made, crispy-on-the-outside, fluffy-on-the-inside, just-the-right-kind-of-greasy, mouthwateringly delicious chips?"

"US!" everyone replied at once.

"But," said Joe, "only if they're MONSTER-sized."

Save some for us, Joe!

Yum!

# ENTER OUR MONSTERCHEF COMPETITION

Visit **www.monsterandchips.com** and create your own revolting recipe to be the Monsterchef of the Year

## Fabulous prizes to be won!